Lucky Star that shines so bright,
Who will need your help tonight?
Light up the sky, it's thanks to you
Wishes really do come true . . .

Lucky Stars

Explore the sparkling world of the stars at
www.luckystarsbooks.co.uk

Wishes really do come true

Lucky Stars

The Ice Skating Wish

Phoebe Bright

Illustrated by Karen Donnelly

MACMILLAN CHILDREN'S BOOKS

A Working Partners book

Special thanks to Maria Faulkner

First published 2013 by Macmillan Children's Books
a division of Macmillan Publishers Limited
20 New Wharf Road, London N1 9RR
Basingstoke and Oxford
Associated companies throughout the world
www.panmacmillan.com

ISBN 978-1-4472-3656-6

1 3 5 7 9 8 6 4 2

A CIP catalogue record for this book is available from
the British Library.

Printed and bound by CPI Group (UK) Ltd, Croydon CR0 4YY

With thanks to all the magical people
in my life for their belief in me

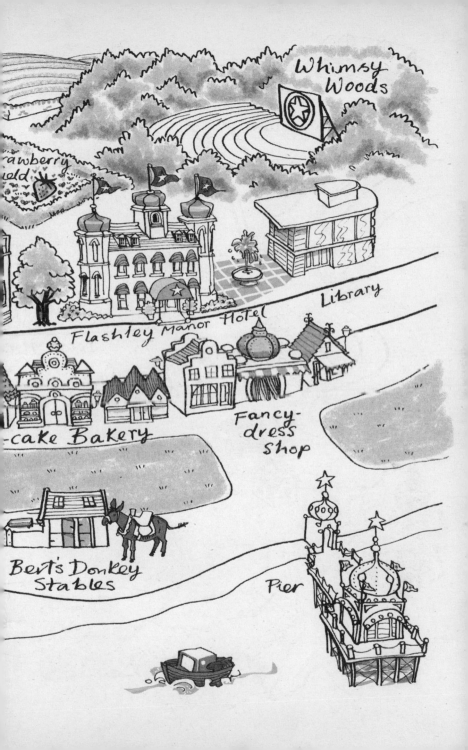

Contents

Hello, friend!

I'm Stella Starkeeper and I want to tell you a secret. Have you ever gazed up at the stars and thought how magical they looked? Well, you're right. Stars really do have magic!

Their precious glittering light allows me to fly down from the sky, all the way to Earth. You see, I'm always on the lookout for boys and girls who are especially kind and helpful. I train them to become Lucky Stars – people who can make wishes come true!

So the next time you're under the twinkling night sky, look out for me. I'll be floating among the stars somewhere. Do give me a wave!

Love from
Stella x

1
Sleepover Friends

The morning sun shone through the domed glass panel of Cassie's bedroom ceiling at Starwatcher Towers.

Sleepily, Cassie rolled over. She loved snuggling under her starry bedcover in her cosy bed. But today something was different . . .

She wasn't lying in her bed!

Cassie opened her eyes wide. She was lying on the floor in a nest of blow-up

mattresses, duvets and sleeping bags. Her
friends, Alex, Kate and Hannah, were
curled up in a row next to her. Tucked
between them was her old cat, Twinkle,
and Alex's fluffy white puppy, Comet.

Last night she'd had her first ever
sleepover.

It was so much fun! Cassie thought,

smiling. *And I made Hannah's wish to have her first sleepover come true.*

Like Cassie, Hannah was a Lucky Star, who could grant wishes. Cassie looked at her friend's hand resting on top of the duvet. On Hannah's wrist her magical charm bracelet glittered in the sunlight.

Cassie looked at her own wrist, where her magical charm bracelet usually shone brightly, and her tummy fluttered with worry. She had lost the bracelet and its seven magical charms at the beach yesterday. She and Alex had managed to find one charm, but

the bracelet and the others were still missing – which meant that Stella Starkeeper's magical powers were fading! Stella lived in the Starry Sky and had helped Cassie to become a Lucky Star.

'I've got to find my bracelet so Stella can get her magic back!' Cassie whispered to herself. Stella had told her to find two Lucky Stars and grant their wishes. Then she could ask them to share their magic and help find her bracelet. *Yesterday I found Hannah at Jupiter Farm*, Cassie thought. *But where will I find my next Lucky Star?*

Alex's eyes blinked open.

'Good morning,' he said, putting his glasses on. 'Is it time to get up yet?'

'Not yet,' Cassie said.

Alex sat up. 'I had a great dream. It was about a scientific experiment I did to get your bracelet back.' Then he looked sadly down at her wrist.

Cassie patted Alex's hand. She knew he was still anxious about her bracelet. He'd been looking after it when it had disappeared. 'Don't worry,' Cassie told him. 'Hannah said she'd share her magic with me.

Now I just need to find one more Lucky
Star and make their wish come true.'

Alex nodded. 'At least we found your star
charm in the sand,' he said.

Cassie touched the little purple charm
hanging on her necklace. It had the power
to take her to other Lucky Stars – and
allowed her to fly.

'I think I'll go and
visit Stella before
the others wake
up,' Cassie said.

'Good idea,'
said Alex.
'I hope
she's all
right.'

'So do I!' Cassie agreed.

Creeping on tiptoes, she quietly pulled the lever that opened the glass panel in her ceiling. She touched the purple star charm and closed her eyes, concentrating hard. *Please let me fly*, she thought.

Cassie opened her eyes. Sparkling stars swirled all around her and excitement fizzed in her tummy as she floated off the floor. Waving goodbye to Alex, she floated through the open window of Starwatcher Towers. Cassie's mum ran a B & B in one part of their home, while her dad worked in the observatory, studying the stars and planets through his telescopes. *But there are some things about the stars even Dad doesn't know*, Cassie thought as she flew higher.

11

Lucky Stars

Far below, the early morning sunshine
lit up the golden sands at the Astral-on-Sea
beach. Some swimmers were already
practising for tomorrow's swimming gala.

Up Cassie soared into the Starry Sky,

higher and higher, until at last she spotted Stella sitting on the little pink star where they often met. Cassie gasped. Poor Stella was even more faded than when she'd seen her last night. Her glorious crown and star-topped wand had almost disappeared, and her silver jacket and dress had turned a dull grey, hanging limply over her colourless leggings and boots.

'Hello, Cassie,' Stella said. Even her voice had lost its sparkle. 'I'm afraid that when your bracelet went missing, it upset the magic in the Starry Sky even more than I thought.'

'I'm so sorry,' Cassie said, giving Stella a hug.

Stella stroked Cassie's blonde hair. 'I

know that you can find your next Lucky Star,' she told her. 'But you'll have to hurry, Cassie. My powers are almost gone, and I won't be able to train any more Lucky Stars . . .'

The Ice Skating Wish

Cassie clenched her fists in determination. 'I won't let that happen,' she said fiercely. 'I'm going to find my bracelet and save you, Stella!'

Stella gave her a faint smile. 'I know you can do it.'

Cassie gave Stella a kiss goodbye and floated back down to Starwatcher Towers.

I've just got to find a Lucky Star today, she thought. *Stella's depending on me!*

15

2
Pancakes and Promises

Cassie floated through the domed window
and into her bedroom. Alex looked up
from his book,
*The Beach
Explorer's Guide.*
'How's
Stella?' he asked.
'Her power's
almost gone,'
Cassie said

sadly. 'I must find my bracelet today.'

'Let's make a plan,' said Alex. 'We'll go out to the shed where it's quiet and use your charm to star travel – just like we did yesterday, when your charm took us to Hannah.'

'Good idea,' Cassie agreed. 'After Kate and Hannah go home.'

'*Yowl!*' Twinkle crawled out from under a blanket.

Kate and Hannah stirred and sat up.

'What's that noise?' asked Hannah.

'Just Twinkle,' Cassie said. 'He wants his breakfast.'

Twinkle pawed

at the bedroom door. When Cassie jumped up and let him out, a delicious aroma drifted up from the kitchen downstairs.

'Mmm,' Alex said. 'My sense of smell tells me that your mum's cooking . . . pancakes!'

'Pancakes for breakfast?' Kate said.

'Yes,' Alex grinned. 'A Starwatcher Towers' speciality.'

'Mum made them when Alex and his parents stayed at the B & B last summer,' Cassie explained. 'She knows they're his favourite.'

'I've heard about Mrs Cafferty's scrumptious pancakes,' Hannah told Kate. 'She's an old friend of my mum.'

'Well, what are we waiting for?' Alex

asked. 'I'm as hungry as Twinkle!'

'*Yup!*' Comet wagged his tail so much he wiggled all over.

'So's Comet,' Cassie giggled.

They raced downstairs to the kitchen,

where Cassie's mum and dad were laying out a huge pile of pancakes smothered in maple syrup.

'Oh, wow!' Alex said.

When breakfast was over Alex patted his very full tummy.

'Four pancakes,' he said. 'That's my mathematical best!'

'Is it scientifically possible for four pancakes to fit in such a small tummy?' Cassie's dad chuckled.

Alex flopped back in his chair. 'Perhaps not,' he said with a groan.

Everybody laughed, including Kate's mum, who had come to walk Kate back to their home at the Fairy-cake Bakery.

'I'll run it off in the garden with Comet,' Alex said. He hurried outside, Comet scampering at his heels. Lazily, Twinkle padded after them.

'Thanks for a lovely time,' Kate said, giving Cassie a hug. 'It was a really fun sleepover!'

They all went to the front door to wave goodbye to Kate and her mum. A big farm truck rattled up the hill and Hannah's mum got out, stomping mud off her wellington boots. While she was chatting to Cassie's mum, Cassie walked Hannah down the path.

'Can you meet me in the Starry Sky tomorrow morning?' Cassie asked.

'At the pink star? Hopefully, I'll have

22

found another Lucky Star by then, so
we can speak to Stella and work out
how to find my bracelet.'

'Of course,' Hannah promised. 'Don't
worry, Cassie. I'm sure we'll find it.'

Cassie gave her a thank-you hug.

'Time to go,' Hannah's mum called.

'Good luck,' Hannah said, 'and thanks for making my sleepover wish come true.'

Cassie ran to the back garden, where she found Alex laughing at Twinkle and Comet. Her old cat was pouncing on a tennis ball and Alex's little white puppy was jumping back and forth, trying to get it back.

'It's great staying here while mum and dad are away,' Alex said.

'It's great to have your help,' Cassie replied. 'Come on! We need to find my next Lucky Star.'

They left Twinkle and Comet playing with the tennis ball, and ran to the shed at the bottom of the garden. They could use Cassie's charm there without being seen.

'I hope it works again,' she said, taking Alex's hand so he could star travel with her.

Cassie closed her eyes and concentrated hard on the charm. *Please take me to the second Lucky Star*, she thought.

At first nothing happened. Cassie

concentrated even harder, and then . . .

'It's working,' Alex said.

Cassie opened her eyes. The garden
was spinning round them and, with a great
swirl of sparkling stars, it began to fade
away . . .

The Ice Skating Wish

Cassie grinned with excitement. *I wonder where it will take us this time*, she thought.

3
The Galaxy Games Centre

The whirling stars cleared. Cassie and
Alex weren't in the garden any more
they were in a busy city square, outside a
huge crescent-shaped building. Cars and
trucks roared past and crowds of people
hurried by. It was much noisier than
Astral-on-Sea.

Cassie felt a little bit scared. 'Where are
we?' she asked Alex.

'This is like the city I used to live in,'

Alex said. 'We'd better stick close together so we don't lose one another.'

Cassie looked up at the sign above the sliding doors of the building.

GALAXY

Games Centre... Fun for all the family

'*Arcades, Craft, Ice Skating . . .*' she read beneath it.

'Galaxies are made up of thousands of stars, you know,' Alex said.

Cassie grinned at him. 'It sounds like a good place to find a Lucky Star! Let's go and look.'

30

The doors whooshed open as they walked into the vast centre.

'This is like the big shopping mall my mum used to take me to,' Alex said.

He led the way to the glittering escalators that connected all the floors. They peered upwards. On the floor above, Cassie could see arcades that reminded her of the one on the pier.

'Wow,' Alex said. 'Look at that ice rink down there.'

Cassie looked down. On the bottom floor, she could just make out little figures skating around the shimmering ice.

There was a crackling sound as the public address system came on. '*Ladies and gentlemen,*' the voice announced, '*don't miss*

our special event at the ice rink this afternoon: Skating Stars!'

'That sounds like fun,' Alex said.

Cassie nodded. 'We should find the second Lucky Star first,' she reminded him. 'Come on – let's keep an eye out!'

They walked along to where a group of
kids was doing activities. A boy cheered
as he threw a foam planet into a basketball
hoop marked 'The Black Hole'. A girl gave
him a high-five.

'No Lucky Stars here,' Alex said.
'They're not wearing charm bracelets.'

Further on, a young woman was painting
children's faces. Cassie saw an older boy in
a baseball cap help a smaller boy on to the
stool.

That was a nice thing to do, Cassie thought.
Could he be a Lucky Star? She looked
hopefully at the older boy's wrist.

'No bracelet,' she sighed.

'I have an idea,' Alex said. 'Let's look at that
map – there, next to the Space Ball Pool.'

He led the way to a large map mounted on the wall. It showed everything in the Galaxy Games Centre.

'There's an Arts and Crafts floor,' Cassie said. 'I wonder if a Lucky Star would go there ...'

'Hey,' said Alex, pointing at the map, 'look at this –'

But Cassie's attention was caught by a little girl and an elderly lady, rushing past. The lady's purse fell from her coat pocket, and Cassie ran to pick it up for her.

'Thank you, dear,' the lady said.

'You're welcome,' Cassie replied.

The little girl was peering out from what Cassie thought was a bright yellow cap. But when she looked more closely she saw that it was the beak of a penguin outfit!

'I wonder why she's wearing that,' Cassie said to Alex.

But when she turned round, Alex was nowhere to be seen!

Cassie's heart beat faster. She'd lost Alex! She peered at the people bustling around her, then saw a boy with brown curly hair getting on the escalator. *There he is,* Cassie thought with relief. *He must have thought I was following him.*

Cassie quickly caught the escalator up to the Arts and Crafts floor. At the top of the escalator the boy turned round.

Cassie gasped. It wasn't Alex at all!

Her stomach did a nervous flip-flop. But then she spotted another curly-haired boy going into a pottery-painting shop.

Oh, good, Cassie thought, running after him. But he wasn't Alex either.

Tears welled up in Cassie's eyes.

This is awful, she thought. *If only I had my charm bracelet — then I could make myself invisible and fly around searching for him . . .*

'Can I help you?'

Surprised, Cassie looked over at a table where a girl about her age was looking up at her. The girl was sitting with a group of friends. She wore jeans and a pink shirt with silver stars on the sleeves, and in her hand was a mug that she was painting. She tucked her black satiny hair out of the way as she put the paintbrush back in the jar.

She's painted silver stars on the mug, Cassie thought. Seeing the star pattern made her feel hopeful.

'Would you like to join us?' the girl asked.

Cassie sat at the table. 'I'd love to,' she said, 'but I've lost my friend, Alex. He's

about my height with brown curly hair
and glasses. I thought I saw him come in
here.'

The girl asked her friends if they had seen
Alex. Nobody had.

'It's OK. I'll help you look,' the girl said.
'I'm Yasmin, by the way.'

'Cassie,' Cassie said with a relieved smile.
'That's very kind of you.'

Yasmin picked up a large white bag and
said goodbye to her friends.

'Bye, Yasmin,' they called. 'Good luck
for later on!'

'Oh, OK, thanks,' Yasmin replied with a
worried frown.

'Why do you need good luck for later
on?' Cassie asked.

'It's nothing,' Yasmin said. 'Come on, let's find your friend.'

As Yasmin swung her bag on to her shoulder, her sleeve rose up her arm.

Cassie's eyes widened. On Yasmin's wrist glittered a charm bracelet covered with seven little charms. Her heart lifted.

I've found my second Lucky Star! she thought.

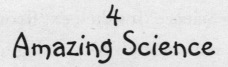

4
Amazing Science

Cassie followed Yasmin out of the pottery-painting shop, wondering what her wish would be. *If I can grant it,* Cassie thought, *I can ask Yasmin to share her magic so I can find my bracelet. But first it's Alex we need to find . . .*

'What does Alex like doing?' Yasmin asked.

'Well, he's very scientific,' Cassie said.

Yasmin grinned. 'I bet he's gone to

Amazing Science. It's the next floor up.'

Cassie remembered Alex trying to show her something on the map. *It was probably Amazing Science*, she thought.

Cassie followed Yasmin on to the escalator. As they went up, she noticed bright orange posters on the walls, advertising the Skating Stars show. The posters included a picture of a girl, her black satiny hair spinning round her as she twirled on the ice.

'That's you!' Cassie said to Yasmin. 'You're in Skating Stars. You must be an amazing ice skater.'

Yasmin fiddled nervously with her hair. 'Er, yes, well . . . Here we are,' she said, stepping off the escalator.

Cassie was puzzled. Why didn't Yasmin want to talk about Skating Stars?

Yasmin led Cassie to an area where kids were doing scientific experiments.

'Amazing Science is truly amazing,' Cassie said as she shook a robot's hand. 'Alex would love it. I'm sure we'll find him here!'

The girls searched around a table where kids were making green slime and a garden of colourful crystals.

But where is Alex? Cassie wondered.

Suddenly, she heard a familiar voice just behind her.

'When you mix the baking soda with the water and lemon juice, it makes bubbles . . .'

'Alex!' Cassie said, spinning round.

There he was, grinning back at her. He was helping a younger boy and girl make lemonade. It was the same little girl in a penguin costume.

Cassie gave Alex a big hug.

'When I realized I'd lost you, I guessed the most logical thing was to wait where I'd

said I was going,' Alex said. 'Because I'd pointed out Amazing Science on the map, I knew you'd find me!'

'I couldn't have found you without Yasmin,' Cassie said, introducing her new friend.

'Hi, Yasmin!' the little girl in the penguin suit squealed.

Cassie and Alex looked puzzled.

'This is Emily,' Yasmin explained. 'She's in the Penguin Club for the younger ice skaters.'

'Yasmin teaches us how to skate,' Emily said.

'Perhaps I could teach you how to squeeze lemons,' Yasmin said, pointing to Emily's messy pile of lemon halves.

'Oh, yes please,' Emily said with a chuckle.

While Yasmin helped Emily, Cassie whispered to Alex that Yasmin was the second Lucky Star.

'That's great,' Alex whispered back. 'Has she made her wish?'

'Not yet,' Cassie replied. 'Look, Yasmin and Emily have finished making the lemonade!'

Alex picked up the jug and poured the bubbly liquid into four glasses.

'Are you going to watch Skating Stars?' Emily asked Cassie and Alex. 'Yasmin's a brilliant ice skater. When I'm a big girl, I want to skate in the show just like her.' She drank her lemonade in two big gulps and skipped off.

Splash! Yasmin's cup of lemonade fell out of her trembling hands.

'Oh no!' said Yasmin.

'It's OK,' Cassie said. 'We can clear it up.'

But Yasmin's eyes
had filled with tears.

Cassie put an arm
round her. 'What's
wrong?' she asked
kindly.

Alex leaned
over to whisper in
Cassie's ear. 'I deduce
it's something to do
with ice skating.'

'Yasmin, are you worried about the
show?' Cassie asked.

Yasmin nodded. 'When I was practising
yesterday, I fell over in my solo. I'm really
worried I'll do it again. I've never been this
nervous before.'

Cassie sighed. How could she make Yasmin feel better? 'Last summer, Alex and I went on stage with Jacey Day, the pop star,' Cassie said. 'Alex was really nervous, but when we performed it was so much fun.'

Alex agreed enthusiastically.

'I usually love performing,' Yasmin explained. 'But I just keep thinking about falling over, and then I don't want to go on.'

'I think you've got stage fright,' Alex said. 'It's when performers get really nervous.'

'You're right,' Yasmin agreed. 'Oh, I wish I didn't have stage fright!'

Cassie and Alex looked at one another.

49

Lucky Stars

Yasmin had made her wish.

But how will I make it come true? Cassie wondered.

5
Skating Wobbles

Shakily, Yasmin picked up her bag. 'I have to go and practise now,' she said.

'Can we come with you?' Cassie asked.

'Are you sure you want to?' Yasmin replied. 'I might just fall over again.'

'Of course we want to,' said Cassie, and Alex nodded in agreement.

They followed Yasmin all the way to the basement of the Galaxy Centre. A blast of cold air hit them when they got to the bottom.

On the huge glistening ice rink, boys and girls of all ages were skating around. Cassie spotted Emily with other little girls and boys, all wearing penguin suits.

'How sweet,' Cassie said.

Yasmin led them to the tiered seats round the edge of the ice rink. She pulled a pair of skates decorated with glittering silver stars from her bag.

'I'd love to learn to skate,' Alex said.

'So would I,' agreed Cassie. 'I've got my pocket money so I can treat us.' Quietly, she added, 'Maybe if we skate as well we can find a way to make Yasmin's wish come true.'

Cassie paid for the
skate hire, and
Yasmin helped
them put on the
heavy skates.

Some girls
and boys
waved to Yasmin
as they skated by.

'They're going to be in the Skating Stars
show too,' she explained. 'Come on, let's
go and join them.'

Yasmin showed Cassie and Alex how to
walk across the bobbled plastic walkway
to the ice. Cassie's heart raced with
excitement. Like Alex, she'd never skated
before.

Yasmin's skates glided easily over the slippery ice.

'She makes it look so easy,' Cassie said.

'The metal blade allows the skate to slide across the ice,' Alex explained to Cassie. 'But if you lean the blade over a bit, it causes friction, like walking on a gravelly path. Then you can turn or slow down or stop.'

'I thought you said you haven't been skating before?' said Cassie.

Alex blushed. 'I haven't. I read it in a book.'

Yasmin skated by again, then twisted round and skated backwards.

Cautiously, Alex and Cassie stepped on to the ice.

'Right, let's go!' Cassie said. She slid her skate forward.

'Yes, let's!' Alex said, moving a bit more quickly.

But as they began to go faster . . .

Bump! Alex fell down on his bottom. 'Ouch!'

'Oh no!' Cassie said.

She skated over to try to help. Too fast!

Bump! Cassie landed on her bottom next to Alex.

Alex chuckled. 'I guess knowing the science of skating isn't the same as actually being able to do it!'

'Are you OK?' Yasmin asked, skating to a perfect stop.

'Yes,' Cassie said with a grin. She and Alex must look so funny!

'I think I'll skate like this,' Alex said, spinning round on his bottom.

Giggling, Cassie did the same. 'Yasmin,' she said, 'if you fall over again, you could spin like this and pretend it's part of the routine!'

Yasmin was laughing as well. 'I think I will!'

She helped Cassie and Alex over to the railings. 'I'll show you how to skate without

falling over,' Yasmin said. 'Start by holding
the rail and walking. It'll help you get a feel
for your skates on the ice.'

'That's very logical,' Alex said.

They moved slowly along.

'That's great,' Yasmin said. 'Now, arms
out, get your balance and glide.'

She held Cassie and Alex by the hand.
Soon they were gliding along with only a
few wobbles!

'You're a brilliant teacher,' Cassie said to
Yasmin.

'The best,' Alex agreed.

'Thanks,' Yasmin said. 'You two skate
together for a while, and I'll practise
my waltz jump. It's the one that tripped
me up.'

Cassie watched as Yasmin took off from one skate, turned in the air and landed on the other foot.

'Fantastic,' she called out. But Yasmin looked worried again.

Cassie frowned thoughtfully. 'Have you noticed that when Yasmin's showing us what to do she isn't nervous at all?' Cassie asked Alex.

He nodded. 'That's because she's not thinking about it.'

The public address system came on. '*Please leave the ice and take your places in the audience,*' it said. '*All performers in Skating Stars get ready. The show is about to begin!*'

'Oh no,' Cassie said to Alex. 'We haven't worked out how to grant Yasmin's wish. Now we're too late!'

They skated over to speak to Yasmin, but a woman in a green skating skirt and black top was calling the team of skaters together. 'I've got to go now,' Yasmin explained. 'That's Mrs Pearce, our skating teacher.'

Mrs Pearce looked worried. 'Two of our skaters have missed their train,' she said. 'They won't make it in time for the show.'

'But we can't do the star formation without them,' Yasmin said. 'Each line in the star has to have the same number of skaters or it won't work. The show finale will be ruined.'

The faces of the skaters fell.

'What are we going to do?' asked Emily, adjusting the beak on her penguin costume.

Yasmin fiddled nervously with her hair. 'Everything's going wrong,' she said to Cassie and Alex. 'And the show hasn't even started . . .'

Cassie looked at Alex. This was their chance to help Yasmin.

'We'll skate in the show!' Cassie called out.

6
Skating Stars!

Yasmin gave a little twirl of delight. 'Thank you so much,' she said.

'We only learned to skate today,' Cassie told Mrs Pearce, 'but thanks to Yasmin's brilliant teaching we can already glide, turn and stop.'

Mrs Pearce smiled. 'That's perfect,' she said. 'We just need you to move in time to the music at the start, then help make the star formation in the finale.'

Alex grinned. 'We can definitely do that!'

'Right, backstage, everyone!' Mrs Pearce called.

Excitedly, Cassie and Alex followed Yasmin to the changing rooms.

Mrs Pearce found them costumes for the show. Alex wore a black T-shirt with a swirl of stars on the front and Cassie wore a pretty yellow skating dress, decorated with stars.

The performers were chatting excitedly, but Cassie noticed that Yasmin was standing away from the rest of them, the same worried frown on her face.

Yasmin was so confident when she was teaching me and Alex, Cassie thought. *How can I help her?*

Cassie's face lit up. She'd had an idea!

'I think I know how to help Yasmin and grant her wish,' she whispered to Alex. 'When Yasmin showed us what to do she wasn't nervous.'

'True.' Alex nodded.

'So perhaps she can pretend to teach us during the show,' Cassie continued.

'Then she won't worry about her solo,' Alex said.

'Yes,' Cassie replied. 'Maybe it'll stop her stage fright.'

Cassie and Alex explained their plan to Yasmin. Although Yasmin agreed, she still fiddled anxiously with her hair.

'If anything goes wrong, you can always do the bottom twirl!' Cassie added, trying to make Yasmin smile.

It worked.

'OK,' Yasmin said with a laugh. 'I'll pretend to teach you. You never know, it might help.'

I hope so, Cassie thought. *If I don't grant Yasmin's wish, my bracelet will be lost forever, and poor Stella's powers will fade away . . .*

Cassie and Alex waited with the beginner skaters, while Yasmin took her place at the front. She wore a beautiful blue dress covered in silver stars. Her skirt swirled around her and a gorgeous star-filled crown shimmered on her head. In her hand was a star-topped wand.

'She looks lovely,' Cassie whispered.

'*Ladies and gentlemen!*' came the announcement on the loudspeaker. '*Welcome to the Galaxy Games Centre ice rink. It's time for our show, Skating Stars!*'

The audience cheered and then went quiet as spotlights swirled over the ice.

Cassie could see the rows of spectators in the audience and her heart raced. She looked at Yasmin, waiting in her solo spot, and waved. Next to her, Alex gave Yasmin a thumbs up.

The lights came on and the music blared. Yasmin spread her arms, tilted her head and smiled. Without hesitating, she skated across the ice, spinning and leaping, her skirt twirling round her.

The Ice Skating Wish

Holding hands, Cassie and Alex followed the other skaters on to the ice. Cassie felt a thrill as the audience clapped in time to the music.

'One, two, one, two,' Alex counted, keeping them both in time.

Yasmin smiled encouragingly at them and waved when they needed to turn, as if she was teaching a class. She didn't seem nervous at all.

'It's working,' Cassie whispered to Alex. 'Yasmin hasn't got stage fright.'

The music got faster and Yasmin skated more quickly around the ice. Cassie and Alex watched as she launched into the waltz turn. But, as she landed, her skate slipped. Cassie watched in horror as Yasmin fell over!

7
Strange Sparkles

Cassie held her breath. Then she saw
Yasmin spin on her bottom, leap to her feet
and hold her arms out in a graceful pose.

Cassie smiled at Alex with relief. Yasmin had made the bottom spin look as if it was meant to be a part of her ice dance!

The finale music began and Cassie and Alex linked up with their line of beginners and made the star shape, skating round and round, with Yasmin in the middle.

When the show was over, Yasmin took a bow. The crowd roared. Then the rest of the skaters bowed too, and the audience cheered some more. Cassie was fizzing all over with happiness.

'Well done, you two,' Yasmin said, skating over to them.

'You were fantastic!' Cassie said.

'Yes, you were,' Alex agreed.

'I didn't have stage fright at all,' Yasmin said. 'Not even when I slipped. Your plan worked – and that bottom spin is really fun! Thank you. You both helped make my wish come true!'

Cassie, Alex and Yasmin sat together to take off their skates.

'I love helping,' Cassie said. And in a serious voice, she added, 'All Lucky Stars love to help.'

She held out her little star charm. It sparkled in the light from the arena.

Yasmin's eyes opened wide in amazement. 'You're a Lucky Star too? I've never met another Lucky Star before!'

'I *am* a Lucky Star,' Cassie said, 'but I've got a problem and I need your help.'

She told Yasmin how she had lost her
bracelet.

'Stella Starkeeper trained me as a Lucky
Star,' Cassie explained. 'But now her
powers are fading because of my missing
bracelet. To find it, she said I have to make

two Lucky Stars' wishes come true.'

'Well, you've certainly done that for me,'
Yasmin said.

Cassie took a deep breath. 'Will you
share your magic to help me find my
bracelet and save Stella?' she asked.

Yasmin smiled. 'Of course I will! Just tell
me what I can do.'

'Yesterday I met Hannah, another Lucky
Star,' Cassie explained. 'We're going to
meet Stella at the pink star in the Starry Sky
tomorrow morning. Then we'll work out
how to find my bracelet.'

'Good idea,' Yasmin replied. 'I know
where the pink star is. I'll see you there. I
can't wait!'

Cassie and Alex said goodbye, then got

changed and returned their skates before walking behind the seating area, where they were hidden from sight.

Cassie took Alex's hand and concentrated hard on her star charm again, calling on its power to take them home. A great swirl of sparkling stars spun round them.

Whoosh! The Galaxy Games Centre began to fade. A few moments later, Cassie and Alex were back in the garden of Starwatcher Towers. Comet was still jumping about, trying to get the tennis ball from Twinkle.

'It's amazing how time stands still when you use star travel,' Alex said. Then he gave a big yawn.

'We were up quite late last night at the sleepover, weren't we?' Cassie said. 'I think I need to copy Twinkle and have a catnap if I'm going to train for the swimming gala this afternoon.'

'Well, scientists say a daytime nap is worth hours of sleep,' Alex said.

Cassie laughed. Alex could come up with a scientific fact about anything!

Later that day, Cassie walked back from her swimming practice at the beach with her friend Danny.

'I'm so excited about the swimming gala,' Danny said. 'I'm really going to try to win my race. I've spent ages practising!'

Tring-tring!

'Mind out!' a screechy voice shouted.

It was Donna Fox, ringing the bell on her bike. Cassie and Danny jumped out of the way as Donna screeched to a halt in front of them.

'You nearly made me tear my dress,' Donna said, scowling.

It was covered in dazzling turquoise sequins. 'Do you like it?' she demanded.

'It's a nice dress,' Cassie said politely.

'It's new, just like my

84

brilliant bike,' Donna boasted.

Donna's parents owned Flashley Manor, the poshest hotel in Astral-on-Sea, and she was terribly spoilt.

'Are you going to the beach to practise your swimming for tomorrow's gala?' Danny asked her.

'I don't need to practise any more,' Donna said. 'My front crawl is amazing.'

Danny's face fell.

How strange, Cassie thought. *I'm sure Donna wasn't that good when I saw her swimming yesterday. Maybe she's just boasting again.*

'I think I'll get off home,' Danny said to Cassie. 'See you tomorrow.'

He walked away.

'I'd better go too,' Cassie said.

'Wait a minute,' said Donna, moving her bike in front of Cassie. 'I want to ask you something.'

Reluctantly, Cassie stood still.

'Do you remember at Christmas, when it snowed and you found that puppy?'

Cassie nodded.

'You had those dog treats in your pocket – just like magic,' Donna said.

Cassie felt uncomfortable. That was months ago. Why was Donna talking about this now?

'I noticed some strange sparkles floating around them,' Donna said.

Cassie swallowed. Donna was staring hard at her.

86

'I just wondered if they were—' Donna
continued.

'It must have been the sunlight reflecting
off the snow,' Cassie said hastily.

'Really?' Donna said. With a shrug, she
turned her bike round and cycled down the
promenade.

A horrible worrying feeling grew in
Cassie's tummy. She had used her charm
bracelet to make the dog treats appear, and
the sparkles Donna saw had been magical.

Could Donna have found out about her magic?

There's no point worrying about it now, Cassie decided as she walked home. *I've got to concentrate on helping Stella.*

She opened the front gate to Starwatcher Towers. Twinkle greeted her with a loud miaow and Cassie picked him up.

'I can't wait for tomorrow,' she told Twinkle. 'Hannah, Yasmin and I will find my charm bracelet, and Stella will be OK again.'

Tring-tring!

From somewhere in the distance came the sound of Donna's bike bell.

'At least I hope that's what happens,' Cassie added as she closed the gate behind her.

Cassie's Things to Make and Do!

Join in the Lucky Stars fun!

Nice Ice Moves

I hope you enjoyed my ice skating wish
as much as I did! Now let's see how
many ice skating moves you know.
Can you tell me which
of the moves below
are real figure skating
moves and which have
been made up? Hint:
there are four made-up
moves.

Double axel   Bird jump

Pancake sit spin   Butterfly spin

Flying lutz   Rabbit hop

Spread eagle   Teapot

Flying camel   Half-cherry salchow

Spot the Difference

Have a look at the two pictures below.
Can you spot five differences?

Ice Skating Party

Why don't you make your very own ice skating wish come true? Invite all your friends to the ice rink and see if everyone can come up with great routines. Do make sure you have permission from your parents and that you have adult supervision at all times.

★ Invite all your friends to the ice rink on a weekend afternoon – with the permission of everyone's parents.

★ Once you have your skates and are allowed on the ice rink, each of you has twenty minutes to make up your very own routine – you can either sing along or make up a routine to the music already playing. You can do this in pairs or groups if you prefer.

★ Once you've made up your routine,

have everyone stand at the side of the
ice rink (being careful not to get in the
way of other skaters) and watch each
person perform.

★ Then ask the parent or parents who
have come with you to judge the best
routine.

★ When the winner is announced, you can
hold an awards ceremony. Draw round
and cut out the trophy on the opposite
page to use for a prize.

★ Good luck!

Answers

Don't look unless
you're really stuck!

Spot the Difference

Nice Ice Moves

The half cherry salchow, rabbit
hop, bird jump and flying lutz
are all made up!

Wishes really do come true

Lucky Stars

The Sleepover Wish

If you missed The Sleepover Wish you can turn the page to read the first chapter now!

1
Lost!

It was a hot summer's day in the seaside town of Astral-on-Sea. Cassie and her best friend, Alex, were at the beach, where the sea sparkled in the warm sunlight and children splashed in the gentle waves.

Cassie was helping Alex to identify shells using a book from the library called *The Beach Explorer's Guide*.

'I think this is a cockle,' she said, holding up a pretty beige-and-white shell.

As she passed it to Alex, the charm bracelet on her wrist jingled. Cassie looked at the seven charms glistening brightly in the sunshine. She smiled, remembering

how her friend Stella Starkeeper had given
her the bracelet. Cassie had earned the
charms by helping to make wishes come
true. Each charm gave her a magical
power – the bird charm allowed her to
fly, and the heart gave her a perfect
memory! Most special of all was the star
charm, which Stella gave her when she
became a Lucky Star. Now Cassie could
grant wishes whenever she liked!

She looked over at Alex, who was busy
inspecting the shell. He was the only other
person who knew about her magical charm
bracelet.

'This cockle is an excellent specimen,'
he said, his dark curly head bent over
the book.

Nearby, Alex's fluffy
white puppy was
digging holes.

'*Yup! Yup!*' barked
Comet, scampering
over with a shell.

'I think he's trying to help,' Cassie
laughed.

'Good boy, Comet,' Alex said.

Cassie patted the wriggly puppy. She was
so glad Alex and his family had moved to
Astral-on-Sea for good. They first became
friends last summer when Alex had stayed at
her parents' cliff-top bed and breakfast.

'Well, I must get on with my training,'
she said, putting her blonde hair in two
bunches. 'The swimming gala is only two

days away and I'd better practise if I want a
chance of winning a race.'

She took off her shorts and pulled her
T-shirt over her head, making the bracelet
jingle again. She wondered what to do.

*I don't really want to swim with my bracelet
on*, she thought. *What if it slips off in the sea?*

'Alex, would you look after my charm
bracelet while I go for a swim?' she asked
her friend.

'Yes, of course,' he replied. 'I know how
special your bracelet is.'

Cassie placed the bracelet carefully in the
pocket of her beach bag.

'Thanks, Alex,' she said, and ran down to
the area roped off for the swimming gala.
Bright orange floats bounced around in the

water as some of the little children practised swimming.

Cassie waved to her friend Danny, whose black hair glistened with water as he swam along.

'Out of the way!' a screechy voice shouted.

Oh no, Cassie thought. *It's Donna Fox.*

Donna swam past Danny, splashing water everywhere. Spluttering, he blinked the water out of his brown eyes.

The Sleepover Wish

'Make way for the best swimmer in Astral-on-Sea!' she cried.

Donna stood up and pulled off her swimming hat.

'Do you like my new swimming costume?' she asked Cassie. 'It's just like the ones swimmers wear in the big races on TV. Mum said I've got to have the best!'

Cassie sighed. Donna's parents owned Flashley Manor, the most expensive hotel in Astral-on-Sea, and Donna was always showing off about her new things.

'I'm going to win the swimming gala,' Donna sneered, flicking her long hair. 'And I'll do whatever it takes.'

Cassie watched Donna march off up the beach.

'Ignore her,' Danny said to Cassie. 'Come on, let's swim together.'

For a while, Cassie swam happily with Danny. Then all of a sudden she felt a jolt go through her. It was kind of like the tingling feeling she got when she used her magic charms, but this didn't make her excited. It made her very worried. Then she felt her wrist go cold.

My bracelet! she thought. *Has something happened to it?*

Cassie called goodbye to Danny and

swam quickly to the shoreline. She ran
up the beach to where Alex was calmly
identifying shells with his magnifying glass.

'Look at these beautiful
mussels,' he said,
holding out the empty
shells with their
glistening blue surface,
but Cassie searched inside
the pocket of her bag
instead. The bracelet was
not where she had put it.

'Alex,' she said
nervously, 'did you
move my bracelet?'

'Er, no,' Alex replied. 'Why would I do
that?'

11

Cassie pointed to her bag. 'It's gone,' she said.

'Gone?' Alex gasped, looking at her. 'But it was right there. Are you sure?'

Carefully, Cassie emptied everything out of the bag. The bracelet wasn't there. She blinked back tears.

'Don't worry, we'll find it,' said Alex, searching among his shells. 'We've got to!'

Cassie checked the rug while Alex looked in the sand around it. But her bracelet wasn't anywhere to be found.

'I – I'm so sorry, Cassie,' Alex stammered. 'I was so busy looking at shells that I forgot about your bracelet . . .'

12

'What am I going to do?' asked Cassie
anxiously.

Comet whimpered and licked her
hand.

Alex thought for a moment. 'Bert came
by with his donkeys while you were
swimming,' he said. 'Let's ask him if he
found anything.'

'Good idea,' Cassie agreed.

They sprinted down the beach to where
Bert was walking the donkeys. His brown
face crinkled into a smile, but when Cassie
told him about the bracelet he just shook
his head.

'You could ask Kara,' he said. 'She's
sunbathing just over there.'

Cassie and Alex ran to where a woman

13

with spiky pink hair was lying on the
beach.

'No, I'm sorry. I haven't seen a charm
bracelet,' said Kara.

Head down, Cassie walked back to the
rug.

'Perhaps Comet buried it by mistake,'
said Alex. 'You could ask him.'

Cassie shook her head. 'I can't,' she said.
'I need my crescent-moon charm to talk to
animals.'

Alex looked thoughtful. 'Do you
remember in Whimsy Wood when you
used your cupcake charm to make us
invisible?'

Cassie nodded.

'And then you used your flower charm

to make something appear?' said Alex.

Cassie nodded again.

'Well, you couldn't actually see the charm bracelet then,' Alex explained. 'But the magic still worked.'

Cassie's heart lifted a little. Maybe she didn't need the bracelet to use its magic. She concentrated hard on the crescent-moon charm and  waited. Nothing happened. No familiar tingling or shower of glittery stars.

Comet yupped quietly.

'What's he saying?' asked Alex.

'I don't know,' Cassie replied sadly. 'I can't understand him. Now I've lost my bracelet, my magical powers have gone too!'

Wishes really do come true
Lucky Stars

Cassie is training to become a Lucky Star –
someone who can make wishes come true!
Follow her on more exciting adventures as
she meets new friends in need of help.

www.luckystarsbooks.co.uk